The Side Hustle

By: Kalyn Metz Knight

The island seemed strangely calm after the violence that had just spread our ship across the white sand. It was still swelteringly hot even though the cover of night enveloped our current surroundings. My eyes seemed extremely heavy and unfocused. I was unable to even tell if my newly found friends were nearby. I should have thoughts. My brain should be racing. Instead, I just have a pounding in my empty head. The warm gooey feeling was unexpected as I started to push my hair out of my face. I pulled my hand down to try to see what was there but instead smelled the mixture of blood and salt. I could feel the grit from the sand in the wound. Then the unbelievable pain hit all at once. I couldn't even tell where it was coming from; it was just all over my body.

'Get it together' popped into my brain. Finally, I was able to form a thought. 'Now slowly... Sit up a little. Steady yourself with your hands.' It took a minute for my body to react but sluggishly I started moving. The sand washed out from beneath my fingers as the tide from the ocean completed its ebb and flow. I took a second to let my eyes come into focus, but the cover of darkness kept me from making much out. Every motion I made took a great deal of effort. I managed to reach my right hand to my left wrist and push the button on the side of my apple watch. Nothing happened. No light. No sound. Just disappointment. 'Duh. That was stupid.' A phrase that had entered my mind many times before. Did I really think my watch would work when the ocean had just swallowed me whole? My brain most really be delayed. Water and electronics don't mix.

"Hello" I managed to get to my feet and call out for anyone really. I had many people in mind, but I didn't care who answered. I just needed to not be alone.

"owweee" I heard a whimper but was unable to distinguish where it had originated. I had hope it was someone from our cruise. It would be even better if it was someone I knew.

“Keep making noise. I am trying to find you” I felt like I was screaming but this may not be true my entire perception was off. I just had hope that whoever whimpered heard me.

As I continued following the whimpers, I felt the sand become hard on my feet. A few more steps and then thud my face was in the sand and I could feel the warmth of another body underneath me. ‘Please don’t be dead. Please don’t be dead.’ Ran over and over in my head as

I slowly began to rise. I sat there a moment plotting my next move when I finally felt movement beside me.

"Ohh.. What, Where, umm" the garbled confusion was exactly what I expected after my own experience waking on the beach. My thoughts were finally starting to come at a normal pace. Who knows how long that had taken? The voice was one I recognized. Cheryl was Mr. Tom's assistant and a leader in the company.

"Take it easy. You will orient yourself after a few minutes." I spoke softly, or at least I think I did, in case she had the same pounding headache I did. It was still there but the joy of finding other people pushed this to the back burner for now. My hand slide deep into the sand as I steadied Cheryl. She began talking but I couldn't focus on her words. I was suddenly very conscience that my hand was not only deep in the sand but on top of warm human flesh. I assumed it was another person's hand but couldn't be sure at this point. I began tapping it.

"Hey, I'm asking what we do now. This isn't time for you to ignore me." Cheryl was almost yelling but I think it was more out of fear than frustration. Her hair was still perfectly in place and she barely had a scrape on her. She was very beautiful even after all we has just been through.

"There is someone else here. Down in the sand. I feel them." I turned over and began furiously digging in case their face was buried. The pile of sand began to shift as Mr. Tom and Shannon both sat up at the same time. As I looked down the beach, I could see probably 15 or 20 other people begin to move. All of which were scared and confused. A muddle of noise rode louder as everyone spoke at once.

"Who" "How" "Where"

"TOOOMMMM" "SARA" "What now"

I couldn't distinguish one voice from the next or even judge the distance from my current location.

"Quiet. I know were panicking but we have to make a plan" I screamed. All the sudden I felt my head spinning and my vision blur back out. Thump! My body was in a lifeless crumple back in the sand from which it had earlier rose.

The light burned my eyes as they begin to flutter. The sounds of leaves rustling and sticks breaking surrounded me. The island was much livelier than it had been last night. People were moving about everywhere. My brain was once again failing to process all that went on. It was only as I tried to sit up that I discovered the leaves fastened in a roof like structure over my head.

"What? Last night everyone was... and Now?" more garbled confusion flowed from my lips but not directed at any one person. "At least I think it was last night."

"Hey, you're up" Cheryl replied not answer my questions but as least acknowledging my existence. "We were so worried." She continued as if it was any another day. In fact, everyone is acting rather strange for the trauma we had all been through. I can still see pieces of the ship trapped in the rocks next to the shore. It was completely unsalvageable. We were going to have to find another way home.

I continued out into the "village", for lack of better term, so I can start assessing our situation. Why is everyone acting like this is a vacation? We were shipwrecked. I notice only about half the people are ones I recognize from the cruise. I have no idea where the others came from.

At the bottom of the path, a familiar face came into my line of sight. Shannon was sitting in a makeshift kitchen area watching over the firepit. I stumbled in the sand before finding a place to slide up beside her. I approached with caution because I wasn't fully aware of the current situation. I knew I was missing pieces of memory from the events of the past week.

"Hi, I am glad to see your ok." I spoke softly so the others in the kitchen could not hear.

"Walk out passed the rocks next to the shore and I'll follow soon. We can talk there. Katirna, be careful who you talk to." She whispered and moved over to the fire.

I sat for a minute trying to process all that was occurring. 'Get up. If you stay to long people will wonder' I thought. I shuffled my feet as I pretended to walk aimlessly headed toward the meeting spot suggested by Shannon. It was only as I was climbing over the last rock, I realized my shoes were long gone. I sat hidden from the world in the cave created by the ocean crashing again the rocks eroding them away.

I jumped a little as Shannon entered the space. Either I was zoned out or she had the quietest approach ever. Even thought we had only met in person a few days earlier at port I felt like she was my lifeline to my existence before whatever this was. She seemed to have answers to the questions I didn't even know to ask.

"I am so happy you're ok." She began "I haven't seen Linley or Anette since we got here. How much do you remember? That bump on your head looks nasty." She paused.

"What the hell is going on? I remember a storm and crash. I woke up on the shore in the dark alone. I found a few others and passed back out only to wake up to it being light and people acting like all of this is normal. I don't get it." I was rambling on and on while Shannon looked at me in complete disbelief.

“You don’t remember the pirates or the money?” She was almost shouting.

“Ummm no. How did it get to this point? Why did I do this? Is my side hustle really going to be the cause of my death?” I was in tears as I thought back to the beginnings of what very well could be my end. The day I was truly introduced to my side hustle.

Initial Investment

"Bing." It's the distinctive tone of a Facebook notification. I almost rolled my eyes as I open the invitation. This is one of many I have received this week. I already have invites to a scent party, a nail bar, 2 different clothing shops, and now a jewelry party. Accept. I guess it won't hurt to watch a few videos to help a friend out.

That was the last time I thought about *WOW Jewelry NOW* until a reminder about the event popped up about 2 weeks later. I had already been to the 4 other parties I had been invited to. Sitting watching more videos really seemed like a waste of my time but I promise Kinlynn I'd go. 'Maybe I'll just turn it on while I watch shows tonight' I thought as I headed out the door to work.

It was the worst day. The office was nonstop. My oldest son had hockey practice after work and my youngest loved to go watch. I loaded up the car and we stopped to get dinner on the way. 'Are all moms a hot mess like this?' I almost laughed as I murmured under my breath. Finally, he took the ice and I sat down. My little went back and forth from watching mickey on his IPAD and his brother. This was it. The 2 hours where I would sit and really be in the moment. Watching every turn on the ice while answering mickey questions. Someone this was what recharged me. The one time I felt like I was doing everything correctly as a mom and still getting a break. Being a mom is not for the weak. Practice ended; we loaded up and headed home for bedtime.

At 9 p.m. I received my event notification to log on. My husband was putting the boys to bed and my weekly show had just started so I might as well keep my promise. The first video started, and I turned the volume half down. There were about 25 ladies watching and interacting. After about 15 minutes I was more in tune to Facebook than my show, so I turned off the tv. 'I can catch the rerun this week' I thought. This party was actually fun. After a game of who wore it best, I won a free bracelet. I don't love jewelry, but the social event of the century was happening at my computer. (ok, more like the most adult talk I've had in a couple weeks but still) I was completely hooked; I had a glass of wine in my hand and for the first time in a few years I was buying complete sets of jewelry for myself. Every where you look is information about moms doing selfcare, but this is one of the few times I've willingly participated in something for me.

At the end of the party, our sales representative described all the benefits and perks of working for *WOW Jewelry NOW*. Discounts that would cause you to have the envy of all jewelry collections. Gift cards and bonuses based on your monthly sales. There are even conferences and cruises that allow you to travel to unimaginable places and they are mostly paid for. Who couldn't use a little extra income? Christmas for the kids could be a little bigger. The goals are so easy to meet and the bonuses easy to achieve. It's a newer company so get in while you can before the market is saturated. Build your customer base now and they will always come to you. She was a great salesperson. I suddenly understood why everyone has a side hustle and after a few days I would too.

Now, to be fair, I am not a rash person. I had to mow this over for a few days before I took the leap. I had to evaluate cost of the first kit with the sales required to make a profit. All side hustles have those initial cost it's just about whether there are long term benefits. I needed a unique plan to adapt their business model to so it would be my own. Figuring how to stay relevant while doing what everyone else was should be a challenge but I didn't find it to be so. After a few days and a flurry of messages between the sales rep. and myself I realized I had already invested time and effort well beyond the decision-making process. So yeah, I guess I already decided; I just wasn't aware. I entered the credit card information and clicked submit. I officially had a side hustle.

Let me back up a moment and say this. I didn't singlehandedly make this decision. Anything I do or don't do is for the betterment of my family. I had many conversations with my husband during this time as well. The thing about him is he is always supportive. He understands that I am well educated, and my family is my priority. He told me to do what I think is best and so I did.

I waited over two weeks for my first kit to arrive. I was very nervous. 'What have a done tying up money we could be using?' entered my thoughts almost daily. It was not that we needed the money desperately, but I didn't like having the resources tied up. Finally, on Tuesday morning I heard the ding of the doorbell and saw the truck drive away. As I slowly peeked around the door, I saw a very ordinary looking brown box on the welcome mat.

"I hope the inside is more impressive." I spend a lot of my time speaking aloud to no one in particular. I guess that's normal who knows.

The swift rip of the tape case the sides to fly up and inside was the most stunning hot pink and tiffany blue package I had ever scene. It reminded me of a French top designer hat box from fashion week Paris. 'Oh, I can make a beautiful storage container out of these' I thought. Heart racing out of my chest. I could hear the palpitations in my ears. The edges of the box released their tight grip as I shimmed the lid upwards. My collection had arrived, and it was everything I could have hoped for. Beautiful pieces. Matching combos. I needed to have a launch party right away. I could earn my initial investment back no problem.

My first task was setting up a business model in functional form. I created spreadsheets to measure expenses and profits. My first entry was negative $450 and once again my stomach dropped. It didn't sound like a lot when she was explaining the pricing but now ugh.

"Don't think about it. Too late to worry about now." I was talking aloud to no one again. Now setup a business

Facebook page. I want it to look refined and elegant yet affordable, much like the box the jewelry came in. Let's call it Katrina's Sparkles and Wine. I want it to be relaxing and enjoyably social for people to relate not a pushy car sales lot for jewelry. I used the tiffany blue and hot pink color scheme from the box dripped with black lace and sparkles for glamour. After three hours of working, I finally sent out invites to my opening boutique party. It was time to go pick up the kids from school. I promised myself I wouldn't get so wrapped up all my time with my kids was gone and I still had to complete my day job requirements. Lucky for me my day job was flexible; I worked mostly from home and if deadlines were met no one said much to me. I was quite proud of all I had accomplished I really felt this would be a great contribution and fun for me.

The next week I spent 2-3 hours each night working at my new job. The kids were asleep so it didn't cut into their time and my husband would sit on the couch watching tv while I worked. I put price tags on each of the items and hung them on the display. The hardest part was creating the initial post for the week hyping everyone up for my new adventure. I was a little unsure of what to say so I researched what other consultants had done. This was a family. We were all on the same team. At least this is what was promoted when I signed up.

Finally, party night arrived. At 8 pm I put the kids to bed so I could get ready. Hair. Check. Makeup. Check. Camera. Ready. It was time to start. I clicked live and Facebook showed me there were 33 people watching. I almost squealed. Much better than I thought.

"Hello tonight friends. I am glad you decided to join us. I want this to be a fun little social event where we talk about anything, wine ourselves down, and I show you some great jewelry." I start my speech.

I see a thumbs up from Erika. This was the sales rep who helped me sign up and she was also my team lead.

"I started this adventure after attending one of these parties myself. I never thought I was one of those side hustle type of women, but things change. I hope you will enjoy my passion." Public speaking had never been an issue for me. I would get a few butterflies like the next person, but I really didn't mind it. The fear of not selling anything was enormous. I would never want to waste our family's money. The hour I had planned to stay on quickly turned into 2 and finally as sells stopped coming in, I said good night.

The entire party was a whirlwind. I had no idea if I had broken even for my initial investment. My wine glass was still on the counter. Cheers to a good time but today is business. I printed of the list of sales:

14 necklaces at $15 each, 7 bracelets at $10 each, 5 anklets at $7each, 11 earrings at $5 each, 15 rings at $5 each, 12 toe rings at $5 each, GRAND TOTAL: $505

I write my second entry into my ledger positive $505. Then in the third column a positive $55 populates from the formula. Alright. I did it. I made my investment back. Then I get this sinking in the pit of my stomach. 'Dummy, that was too easy. You forgot the shipping and materials cost.' The thought whizzed into my brain as I rolled my eyes. I order 100 bubble mailers for $35. The total cost of shipping for my first batch was $120. After party one I was negative $100. I still had about 50 pieces of jewelry left. I could have another party and see how that goes. After my second party I'll decide if its worth continuing this journey.

I set up a second party for the following week as a mystery hostess party. This is where everyone who buys something is put in a drawing for "Hostess rewards." Hostess rewards vary from month to month but include free jewelry and discounts depending on the amount sold. The second party was a huge success. At the end of the night there was not one piece of jewelry left and I was $250 to the positive. I was hooked.

From here I started ordering inventory almost weekly jewelry would come and go our garage turned into a makeshift studio and I was hosting lives three nights a week. I kept up with my day job pretty well, but I had let a lot of other things go. After I missed hockey twice and worked in the stands through the game my husband sat me down for a chat.

"Honey, I think we need to talk about this side hustle. I want you to know I appreciate how hard you work but you are starting to take time away from me and our kids. I didn't care at first but when Kevin asked if you saw his goal and you said yes, I know you were lying. I see you more on Facebook than in our home." He was talking very calmly but I was seeing red.

"How dare you! Are you saying I'm a bad mother? I did this for us. Extra money. Remember." I was almost screaming. I got up and ran out of the room. "Shit. I'm not a bad mother. I'm just a hard worker. He has no idea what I've sacrificed over the years. Friendships and promotions. All for him and our kids. This is for me. Damnit. This is mine." The hot tears stung my face mostly because somewhere deep inside I realized he was right. I was obsessed. I did the one thing I promised I wouldn't let happen. I took my kids time to give to my side hustle. I never admitted he was right, but I also never missed hockey again. I would find other time to devote to it.

My third month in business I received a promotion, 3 bonuses and qualified for a weekend trip to Mr. Tom's house. Mr. Tom owned the company. He brought it from the ground up. He made all the designs, picked all the colors, and coordinated all the sales. He was *WOW Jewelry NOW.* I was so excited.

I packed my bags and kissed my husband and kids' bye. I could see them wrestling in the yard as the cab pulled out to the airport. I opened the brochure with pictures of the beautiful ranch next to a stream and the factory in the background. Tennessee was so nice in the fall all the leaves changing colors. It was only about an hour and a half plane ride. There was a car service at the airport to pick us, well me, up. I immediately got an uneasy feeling when the driver said Mr. Tom only invited me to his place this round. Every bone in my body told me to run. To get back on the plane and cut all ties. I didn't. I couldn't. I wanted to be the best of the best at everything I do and if it meant spending a weekend with Mr. Tom so be it. Plus, when we applied, we had to let them know our marital status. Surly he won't try anything. I mean I'm flattering myself anyway. No one wants a tired hot mess of a wife/mother in their 30's. Guys who own companies are already married with mistresses in their 20's or their gay.

I pushed those sick feelings deep to the back of my mind as I exited the car and knocked on the front door. A petite brunet about 18 opened the door. 'I didn't know Mr. Tom had kids' I pondered.

"Hi, I'm Ashleigh, come on in and I'll give you the tour. Mr. Tom will meet us at the factory in just a bit. We will stop and put your bag in your room on the way." She was so polite as she directed me around.

"I was scheduled at the bed and breakfast in town." I replied.

"Mr. Tom will have no such thing. He always allows his guest to sleep in one of his many extra rooms. He has 8." She insisted. "Now your bags will be brought to this room on the left. I'll give you a few minutes to make sure it is to your liking. The bathroom and closet are connected."

I entered what I can describe as only the most refined French perfume bottle of a room. The chandelier had little crystals hanging down from all over, the king size bed was draped in silk, and everything was in the *WOW Jewelry NOW* color scheme. In a weird way there was something familiar about the pillows on the bed. I had never been there before and couldn't put my finger on it. Oh well.

A few minutes more Ashleigh knocked on the door and asked if I was ready to proceed. We walked the house and the grounds. She had so much knowledge almost as a museum curator. Each piece she showed me, each detail she shared made me fall more in love with the property Finally, we went up to the factory.

"Oh, good afternoon my dear. I trust your flights was as lovely as you my dear." Mr. Tom immediately came in for a hug and a kiss on the cheek. He was not at all what I expected. He was maybe 35 or 40 and stood about 5'9 with sandy hair and piercing blue eyes. His t shirt was nothing special and jeans were a bit dusty. I was almost sure he had come straight from the stables to the factory.

"It's nice to meet you Mr. Tom. I am such a big fan of your work. And yes, I love to fly so it was a wonderful trip."

"Did you like the pillows? I pulled the black lace design from your page. You are very good with design yourself" He almost remarked as if looking for approval. 'How odd? I knew I recognized those. Say something simple not stupid' my brain was guiding me thank goodness.

"I love them. I never thought an idea of mine would fit in such a beautiful place." I replied. 'Way to play that cool. Being humble while not stating the weirdness of it all.' I thought to myself as we continued the tour of the factory. He showed me the plan for the future designs, we looked at colors for hours and I even helped make some decisions. Mr. Tom was a very nice man but something in his eyes when he talked about the pillows made me feel sorry for him or concerned. I'm not even sure what the emotion was but there was definitely more to it.

We finished the tour and headed back to the house for dinner. He asked about my life and my family. We shared storied of our many adventures. He was way more exciting than I was. I yawned just as we finished dessert. I excused myself to my room looking forward to a nice long bath in the most elaborate bathtub, I had ever laid eyes on.

“Goodnight Mrs. Katrina, hug the pillows you designed tightly.” Mr. Tom stood as I got up to exit the room.

“Goodnight Mr. Tom” I yawned again and headed for the stars. When I reached my room, I found my clothes put away in the closet and a trolley containing three bottles of wine and a class. The note on the tray read: you usually drink red on your lives, but I pulled a white and a rose just in case. Enjoy! Tom. I pulled my pajamas and my robe from the closet and threw them over the end of the trolley. I wheeled the entire thing into the bathroom. The tub set on a platform in the middle of the room with three steps to enter it. It was a white overside garden tub trimmed with gold claw feet and a gold facet. The tub had custom jets and a rain fall shower head mounted on the ceiling above it. As I turned on the water, I noticed the bottom of the steps were surrounded by a grate to drain the water if you chose to use the shower. As I slumped down in the tub with my wine glass 'who is this man? Why did he tell me to hug the pillow?' ran over and over in my mind. 'I love my husband I am not catching feelings for this man, but I just want to know what his story is' I was almost in a state of confusion when finally, I decided the only way to figure it out was to hug the pillow.

I dried and slid on my robe long enough to make it to the bed. Once I wrapped my arms around the pillow, I felt the tiny pouch almost like a pocket. I cautiously slid my hand in and pulled the piece of paper out. I laid on the silk draped bed holding the note between the pillows. My heart raced as I quietly unfolded the piece of paper. It was hard to see by the candlelight, but I dared not turn on more to draw attention to myself as I could see people shuffling in the courtyard.

The Note

Dear Katrina,

I hope you don't take this the wrong way as I know you are happily married with a family. I watch your page every time you are on and you seem like such a lovely woman. There is a lot going on behind the scenes that I need help exposing. I will get in more detail on the cruise next month, but I truly need your help. My life along with many others are in danger. Meet me at Port Charles Mall at 11:30 am before we board the ship. I will be by the fountain in the courtyard. Don't mention anything here we are bugged.

Thank you in advance,

Tom

I stared at the note in disbelief. 'What the hell? My videos made some guy who has never met me trust me. Am I in the middle of a joke or a game? This entire trip has been filled with eccentric things, but this takes the cake.' These thoughts swirled in my head as I quickly shoved the note back in its secret pocket. Some how I knew this was no game. I suddenly recognized the look I had seen in his eyes when he mentioned the pillows. It was fear. Pure fear. I decided to shove the pillow in my bag and take it home with me. I didn't have to put much thought into this I was going to help.

The next morning, I headed down to breakfast. I had to find a way to let Mr. Tom know I would help without raising suspicions. I had no idea what I was involved in, but I needed to put the clues together when I got home. The sun was shining through the stain glass window creating a glow over the breakfast nook. Mr. Tom was already sitting drinking a cup of coffee with a hug pastry spread in front of him.

"Good morning Mr. Tom; the pillows with my design were fabulously cushioned to sleep on last night. Best sleep I've had in ages." It was an odd thing to say over breakfast, but I think he got the message without raising too many eyebrows.

"Thank you, Mrs. Katrina. I hope you remembered to pack it as a keepsake from your trip." I lightly taped my bag as he was finishing the sentence. We made small talk for the rest of the morning while I munched on the most delicious cheese danish. I remained cool and collected on the outside but inside I was screaming. I wanted to kidnap Mr. Tom and bring him to my house, although not sure my husband will think it's a great plan so maybe a hotel. He walked me to the door just as the car service arrived. I leaned in for a hug.

"See you soon Mr. Tom. Don't worry I'll be live again soon!" I whispered in his ear still afraid I was blowing what ever operation I was now involved with.

"Have a safe flight. Until we cross paths again." He whispered back with a kiss on the cheek. The fear was still detectable in his eyes but for the first time I was also able to see hope. Message received, at least I guess that's what it meant. I waived out the back of the car holding on to hope that I would see Mr. Tom again.

Once I got home, I held my family so tight. My husband could tell something happened; something was different than before I left. He never asked and I didn't offer. I had no desire to bring my family into the dark world of my side hustle. I didn't even know what this dark was, but it seemed dangerous.

I had six *WOW Jewelry NOW* parties over the next two weeks. Each time I went live I would hold my breath until Mr. Tom's name would pop up as a viewer. The first four parties it only took about ten minutes before I could take a breath. The morning of party number five was like every other day. I ran the kids to school, did a few errands, and then checked the mailbox on the way back home. In the mail I recognized the distinctive pink and blue color scheme on one of the envelopes. I slowly slid my finger down the crease of the seal. ‘No. Wait until you get back in the car. They could be watching’ My paranoid thoughts had reached an all time high since I returned from my trip to Tennessee. I tucked the mail under my arm and scurried the short path to the parking lot.

As I sat staring out the windshield, I was very aware of my rapid breath. Once again, I pulled out the pink and blue envelope, but this time I opened it with a bit more haste. The unfurled letter revealed a ticket for a weeklong sail on the Magic Madness. 'This is the cruise he must have been talking about. What does one pack for an operation into a dangerous exposure when they don't know what they are exposing?' I always have the stupidest thoughts in important moments. The letter that accompanied the ticket shed a little light on the cruise.

My Dear Katrina,

CONGRATULATIONS!!!!! You were one of the top sellers for the third region. Join us, the WOW Jewelry NOW staff, and 20 of the countries top selling consultants on a weeklong cruise as a reward. We will stop on a private island for surf and sand. The entire week will be limitless fun. You will also receive your $15,000 top seller bonus while aboard. The ship Magic Madness is one of the most coveted on the seas and its ours for the entire time. Please bring your ticket and you consultant number to Port Charles on Saturday October 7th. The boat will leave precisely at 5 pm. Reply within 3 days to WJN@mail.com in order to claim your spot. Again, Congratulations on your growing success.

Mr. Tom and your WOW Jewelry NOW staff

I had already told my family about winning the cruise, but a week notice was not much time to prepare. My husband fully supported me going since I had been better about my time management with the business. I'm guessing the extra income didn't hurt in his decision as well. I sent the text letting him know I would leave Saturday and headed to pick up the kids.

I couldn't wait for the live tonight as soon as I saw Mr. Tom log in, I would announce my inclusion in the cruise as my way of letting him know I'd still be there. Ten minutes in I begin to watch the names. I couldn't show my concerns as the minutes passed by. An hour later I signed off. No Mr. Tom. I could not let my mind wonder why he didn't long on. I did not want to imagine what horrors waited him. On Friday night, I hosted my final party before the cruise. I again searched for Mr. Tom with no success but just as I was about to sign off a comment popped up from Anonamouse8989: 9 am. No explanation but in my heart, I knew it was him. I spent the rest of my night packing the bag and preparing for whatever we would face.

Beep! Beep! Beep! My alarm was screaming for me to get ready. My stomach was in knots as I said my goodbyes. The boys weren't up yet so a soft kiss on the forehead and a rub on the hair before heading out the door. When I inserted the key in the door to lock it, I felt a great deal of unexplainable sadness. It was the first time I truly feared not seeing my family again. The taxi pulled up and honked so I turned the key and headed off to the Port Charles Mall.

Port Charles

It took about an hour and a half before we pulled into the parking lot at Port Charles mall. It was crowded for this early hour, as the clock on the dash shown 8:48am. I grabbed my luggage and tipped the driver. '10 Minutes until... well... whatever this is.' I thought as I checked in at the cruise line before heading into the mall.

"We will have your luggage placed in your state room. Please return to the ship by 3pm for your departure. We will open for boarding at noon. Thank you for joining our adventure" The mans voice trailed off as I was already turned towards the mall looking for Mr. Tom. I headed down the long, Spanish style corridor with stores on each side, until I saw the veranda in the middle. This area reminded me of ancient gardens with plants and moss hanging from the ceiling. The fountain looked like clay pots spilling into a pool. The beauty was overwhelming.

I spotted Mr. Tom on a bench to the left side of the fountain. He looked to be in one piece, although, I could see a little bruise on his cheek underneath his brown mirrored sunglasses. Once we made eye contact, he nodded his head for me to join him. I surveyed the room for anyone out of place then casually strolled over. He greeted me with a hug and kiss on the cheek.

"Oh Kat. I am so glad you came. The past two weeks have been horrible. I haven't had contact with anyone. I don't know where they are being held. The boss is becoming more aware of my failures. I truly need your help." He was in tears as he murmured the last of his words.

"Mr. Tom, I need you to start at the beginning. Tell me all that is going on and all we need to do." I was still trying to piece together his thoughts.

"Ok." He gathered his composure as he started to explain. "About three months are I started WOW Jewelry NOW I was struggling to keep the company going. I started this company as a gift for my little sister, Alena. I didn't want to fail her. So, when a gentleman named Don approached me about investing, I let him come aboard. At first, I thought he was the perfect business partner. He handled all the cruises and travel and invested around $550,000 a year to keep us going. When I finally decided to join him on one of the cruises, I brought Alena with me. Don was nervous the entire trip; he kept asking me if I was sure I wanted to go into to town when we docked at Copper Bay Island. I got off the ship with Alen and watched as two groups of men entered the ship and unloaded reams of cash and then they placed a bunch of boxes in the cargo hold." I could see the tears begin to fall as he mustered the strength to continue.

"Just take you time and breath. I promise I'm going to help" I reassured him to continue would be worth it.

"As Alena and I approached the Lazy Days bar to celebrate her 10th birthday, three of the men from the ship ran up behind us and put a gun to our backs. They walked us to the back of the bar and informed me they were keeping Alena until I brought them clean money and proof of delivery of the creates. Apparently, Don has been using me, while my business, to clean money for some kind of underhanded dealings. This is where I need you help. I need to get back Alena and find out what is in the crates. These guys, who I know only as B's crew, have been keeping tabs on me since I left Copper Bay. I need my sister back. I need help"

"I'm here. We will figure something out." He hugged me again as I reassured him I would help. I suggested we stroll so not to draw attention to ourselves. We stood up and started slowly back towards the docks. Casual small talk disguised our need to think of a plan when suddenly I had an idea.

"I think we should board at noon. The ship will have just enough people to blend in but not so many as to distract us. We need to find out what is in those boxes before we know our second steps. We need to know today." I was sure this would answer many of our questions.

"Here is the key to my room number 103 on the south deck. It's the suite. We should board separately. I'll meet you there at 1 pm. Go to your room first and make sure it's all good. I'll be waiting." Mr. Tom disappeared back down the corridor we came from. I stood formulating all I had just been told. 'What could these boxes contain? Drugs? Guns? People? It really didn't matter. We had to get Alena back and get these people out of the business.' My brain was swirling. Images of my sons and husband playing in the yard. Alena must have a chance to play again.

I moseyed in an out of a couple stores just to pass time. The port started getting more and more crowded, but I couldn't focus on other people. I needed to get a couple things and eat. Finally, I found a coffee shop to eat a little something while the final minutes passed until boarding. I needed to get in the correct frame of mind which included coffee. 'Ok. Here we go' I thought as I strolled passed the stores and out on to the dock.

The ship was massive. I felt so small standing next to the blue hull of the ship. The line to board already wrapped around two turns in the que set out. At 11:45 I was handed my key and room information: 248 South deck. 'Well at least we are both on the south deck' I thought as I started my journey up the long ramp to the deck. I noted all the signs as I passed looking for not only my room but how to get to Tom's. It seems like one elevator ride up and a long corridor towards the center of the ship was all that separated us. 'I am glad we are not far apart. Wonder if he did that on purpose' Really dumb and useless thoughts were once again entering my head. 248 appear on the wall plate straight in front of me. I pushed the key into the door and felt the click as the lock flung back.

I hesitated, taking a huge deep breath, before pushing the door open. The bright white almost blinded me as the sun flooded the room from the deck. Touches of blue and teal brushed the room on the pillows and in the comforter. There was even a little hammock in the corner of the room overlooking the deck. I stepped outside to smell the sea before returning to put my luggage away. When the last shirt was out in the drawer there was a knock at the door.

"Hello, Mrs. Katrina? I am John. I'll be one of the stewards in this area of the ship. I am just checking to see that your room is up to your standards." He was very polite and soft spoken yet somehow, I couldn't help but wonder if he was one of B's gang.

"Oh yes, John, everything is lovely. I shall most enjoy my week on the ship." I replied. It came out much more sarcastic and overstated than I intended for it to. John looked at me questioning my sincerity before he departed back into the hall. All most as soon as he shut the door a second knock came. I opened the door to see a darked skinned woman with curly brown hair.

"Hello," she smiled "I'm Shannon. I'm in the room next door. Just wanted to introduce myself in case you wanted to do something in our down time."

“That would be fun. I’ll catch up with you this week I’m sure. I’m Kat, well Katrina but mostly Kat.” I replied trying to sound casual and not to eager.

“Cool. See you later” She closed the door behind her.

I turned to go back to the balcony when the clock above the glass doors caught my eye. Already ten until one. I need to make my way to Tom’s room without being noticed. The hallway was a flurry of activity with passengers boarding and staff checking the rooms. I just kept moving along the corridor making polite smiles and little hellos until I reach the elevator up. I quickly noticed a security camera in the left corner, so I tried not to look directly into it. I slipped off at the top deck and took a left down a slider hall. The top floor had much less activity; in fact, I didn't pass anyone on my way. Room 103 was all the way at the end and the only door on this side of this deck.

I raised my hand for a quick knock then remembered what Tom had said at the mall 'Don't knock just come in. I'll know your there.' I turned the key and slid in the door through the smallest of space shutting it quickly behind me.

"WOW" I gasped as I looked up for the first time. Tom's room was elaborate just like his house. There was a beautiful, beaded chandelier over the ornate mocha coffee table, a burgundy coach with old smoking chairs to match, and everything was polished with gold fixtures. It was a sight. I ran my hand along the back of the couch as I walked over to see what was displayed over on the coffee table.

"Have a seat. I'll be right in." Came bellowing from another room in the back corner. As I sunk into the corner cushion of the couch, I realized rolled out across the coffee table was a blueprint of the ship we were currently on. I traced my finger from our current position down three decks, over a bridge in the center veranda, through a corridor running the length of the back of the ship, down a small ladder into the cargo space below the water level.

"Here," I pointed as Mr. Tom sat down beside me. "This would be the most logical place to store the boxes and easily conceal their content from passenger view. It also looks like there is a loading elevator in the back of the room that goes to the dock two floors above." I paused and then a smile drew across my face. "I know how to get there but we are going to need some help. What do you know about Shannon in the cabin next to me?"

"I knew you were a good judge of character" he laughed. "She is a fear friend and already aware of the situation. She is not as well educated, or family driven as you, but she would definitely help with some direction."

"Good. We need her." I retorted. Tom grabbed a small bag with a flashlight and a few other things I couldn't see inside. I figured he would be prepared but he was extremely ready. We made our way to Shannon's room. We decided the best approach was to simply act as if Tom was giving me a tour of the ship making small talk along the way. It only took about ten minutes to descend the elevator and ramble down the corridor. The ship was getting rather crowded as the three o'clock board deadline drew near. Shannon immediately brought us in and squalled with delight.

"Oh Tom, I had a good feeling about her. I knew she'd help." She was very peppy even in the somewhat bleak circumstances we were facing. The ship was already in a full swing party as the final guest boarded. That was good for us; it gave us a lovely cover to explore our way down to the cargo hold.

"Got any liquor. A shot for encouragement followed by these glasses full along with a little stumble down the hallway and I doubt anyone will question where we are going. Just act a little tipsy and keep the party going" I could see the smile draw across their faces as I laid out my plan.

"You're a little sneaky and a lot scary." Shannon winked as she almost laughed the words out.

"Ok. Down the hatch." We all took the shot, slammed the glass on the table, and scurried out the door laughing. The hallway was so crowded we bumped into people with every other step. No one questioned us or even gave us a second thought. We would occasionally be stumbling into each other laughing the whole way. We reached the elevator and entered alone. I put my hand on Shannon's shoulder and leaned over to whisper in her ear.

"Keep it up CCTV in the right corner. We need to be looking as we move through the ship. It's important to have a read on where all the cameras are." We both laughed as if I told her a joke. I made sure to trip on my way out of the elevator.

This deck was not the party that upstairs had been. It was dark and dingey, needed repainted about a century ago, and eerily quiet. It was obvious that only crew should be down here. If someone came by, we would have to be quick on our feet.

“Let me barrow your flashlight a second; I drew a quick sketch on my cocktail napkin of the path we need to take.” I whispered but the echo made it sound loud.

“Look at that. Always thinking a million miles ahead. She really can help us.” Mr. Tom couldn’t contain his excitement. I gave a quick glance back towards him as he quickly dropped Shannon's hand. I was getting the impression there was more to the relationship than they let on, but it really didn't matter. I was invested and I wanted to get Alena back.

"Ok. Once we get to the back of the boat, we should find a stairwell down into the cargo hold." I said as I started slinking toward the back. I heard mumbled voices headed our way. "Time to act again." I whispered. We began laughing and stumbling. As we saw the worker's approach.

"Don't have too much fun." One of them remarked as he passed.

"We are just looking for a little quiet." I teased as I pulled Shannon close in a suggestive manner.

"And we won't hurt him so don't worry" she slushed her drink out as she slurred her words and winked. We both laughed and continued on our way. We could hear the two men snickering and giggling as we reached the ladder. Tom hovered over shinning the flashlight below. I climbed approximately halfway down before jumping to the floor. I almost forgot to wait on Shannon and Tom who shrieked as I took my third step towards the crates. As I turned back, I heard the second thud from Tom's feet hitting the floor.

I picked a group of crates toward the back corner and directed everyone behind them in case we had company. They would provide some cover as we revealed their contents. We squatted next to the middle one and Tom shuffled some things around in the bag.

"Here" he whispered handing me a crowbar and a small disk. "Its GPS to drop in so at least we can track the crate."

"Great idea. How many of those do you have?" I responded.

"About five more" he smiled. "Shannon and I will place them in a couple of these other crates while you open and take pictures. I sat a camera next to your feet."

"Ok but hurry. I figure we have ten- or fifteen-minutes tops before someone wonders in." I was already placing the crowbar underneath the corner of the lid. SNAP the wood splintered a little as the top corner came lose. I looked to make sure no one heard and then stuck the camera under the corner. In the flash from the camera, I thought I saw a glimmer of gold. I repeated the process on three or four more boxes before ushering the others to come on. Just as we reached the top of the ladder two men were standing waiting for us. Panic set in not only in my mind but all over Tom and Shannon's face.

"That is a restricted area. What were you doing down there?" The older man's voice boomed.

I quickly adjust my top and pulled a pair of panties from my pocket. Thank goodness they had gotten caught in my pants leg in the laundry. "Awww, come on.

You can use your imagination. Tom here didn't want the other girls to think he plays favorites." I winked and smiled just as Shannon planted a kiss on Tom's cheek. She wiped her lips and winked at me and we walked. We never looked back and about the time the elevator dinged I finally took a breath. I wanted to laugh or cry; I'm not really sure. My mind was racing but we did not say a word until we made it all the way back to the suite hall Tom was staying in.

"What just happened?" Shannon was the first to speak.

"Wait we are almost in the room." I barked. She was taken back by my tone. I had an idea what was in those crates and it was bigger than I could have imagined. It wasn't drugs, guns, or people. That would have been way to normal. Tom walked ahead an unlocked the door. Every second that ticked by made my heart race faster. I had to process and decompress before I burst. There is no way possible those items were on this ship. It just couldn't be. Finally, the door opened, I ran in a sat on the couch feeling like I was going to pass out. I heard the click of the lock from the door as Tom came over. I wasn't sure where Shannon had disappeared to, but I knew she was in here somewhere.

"I think I saw a ghost. Well at least the possessions of a ghost. It is not possible those items are on this ship." I could tell by Tom's face I wasn't making much sense. "Hand me the camera please." As the picture developed on the screen my knees went week again. I guess we all had some secrets that couldn't be left in the past. These were museum quality antiquities I hadn't seen in 10 years.

The Past was Here.

I don't know if it was something in my eyes or my tone of voice, but Tom could tell I was scared and confused. He wrapped his arm around my shoulder to steady and reassure me. Shannon came from the back room and sat next to me. She put her hand on my leg. We were in this together. It was obvious from their kindness that they understood that whatever I was dealing with had a complex level of difficulty. I gathered my thoughts and decided it would be ok to tell them the story.

"About 12 years ago I was a 22-year-old teaching assistant for Professor Thomas Allen at Homme University. He was a genius in history. He had millions of theories about the development of the world and his collection of artifacts rivaled all the museums." I couldn't help but smile thinking of all the time spent with this man. "He traveled and explored every moment he could. I spent every moment I could listen to his adventures. He was only 35 but had more experiences than most 50-year-olds. Throughout the semester we would teach and explore and eventually I fell in love with this man. I fell hard and so did he. Over Christmas he wisped me to

Egypt and Ireland and Germany where we married in secret. I never changed my name and agreed to stay his TA at work and his wife at home until I could graduate. My final semester of my third year I had to stay and take finals while he went on a trip to Turkey. He was only to be gone for five days but I got a call he had been hit by a mortar during an attack in a town market. He didn't survive." Tears were streaming down my face as I tried to speak.

God, I hadn't thought about Thomas in years because it just hurt too much. All that could have and should have been, stung. I felt like I was wishing away my family now even though I loved them dearly. I love my boys, but my life could have been a grand adventure with Thomas and our kids. It was everything that made me love this man flooding back.

“Anyway, I didn’t know it but when we’d come back from Germany Thomas had added me as his wife and beneficiary to everything. His home. His life insurance and pension. Royalties to all his published pieces. Most importantly his collection of antiquities. I never wanted it. I never asked for it. Just loving that man and being loved by that man was far more than I deserved. He never told me that everything was mine. I have never lived off his money or clued my family into how wealthy we are because I never wanted to make my husband feel less. I have several bank accounts that pay charities and college funds for the kids. I send Thomas's sister money throughout the year and paid for his parents' care until they both passed. The house is now rented to a lovely couple who couldn't afford other. The antiquities... My collection was really the only part of it that could even be remotely traced back to me. I loaned this collection to two different museums; one being at the university and the other where I do my day job. How on earth did these items get on your ship?" The room was silent as I drew a breath. My mind was racing ‘There’s no way the items were stolen, or I would have been notified.’

“I need to make some calls.” Tears again created rivers down my checks as I could barely get the words out. It hurt as much now as it did the day he passed. Shannon went into the other room as Tom and I talked.

“You can stay here tonight I have three bedrooms. I’ll have your stuff brought up from you room. We wouldn’t want you alone.” Mr. Tom’s kindness shown in his warm smile.

"Hold on to her." I remarked "I love my husband. I truly do but losing Thomas is something I will never get over. He was my soul. You have that with Shannon. I see it." I smiled through my tears as a look of pure shock spread across his face.

"I.. I mean.. We.. Sorry we didn't tell you sooner. I am very protective, and I didn't want you to think. I, well, I don't know why I didn't tell you." Mr. Tom stumbled over every word as he spoke. Shannon brought some tea in from the kitchen.

"It's fine Tom. Really. But a love like yours can be seen in every look so hiding it will be very hard for you. Goodnight Tom, Goodnight Shannon." I yawned as I took a sip of the tea and pulled the phone to my ear.

Ding. The sound of my email woke me before 7. 'No heart in the bottom left corner of the tag. No etching under the color. This is definitely a fake but a really good one.' I was perplexed. I knew the collection was worth money but the elaborate scheme to forge pieces to replace with must have taken time.

Dr. Moriss.

Please seal the collection off from the public and keep track of all university personnel who enter the collection until further notice. I also need security to send me all tapes and logs for the collection since January. I know it will take time and I will pay all associated cost. I will let you know the next steps. Please just tell everyone the collection is going through refurb.

Thank you again,

Send. Now to sync the GPS trackers to our computers and phones. I need to know where my collection is always. It feels like my last piece of Thomas. It holds the last of my secret love.

Just as I finished setting them up, I heard a noise from the kitchen.

"Good Morning," I shouted as I rounded the corner. An individual wearing all black ran passed me and out the suite door. He knocked over a vase on the way out.

"TOOOMMMM someone is in here." I screamed but he didn't answer. A steward came in from the hallway.

"Is everything ok?" He said with a great look of concern.

"No! Get Mr. Tom right now." I was still shouting even though I didn't need to. Just then Tom and Shannon came into the door. “Tom, so guy was rummaging through the kitchen. I guess he saw you leave and thought everyone was gone.” I was in tears again. So much for a good vacation; no one cries this much if its good. “I don’t understand he didn’t take anything.”

“Go to the bedroom with Shannon.” Tom was stern but calm. “You guys come with me.” After about ten minutes Tom entered the room. “Your right they were looking for something but didn’t find it. Nothing is missing.” Tom looked a little distressed but tried not to let on. He kept reassuring us it would be fine, and we should go to the dinning room for lunch.

He would stay in the room and by the time we were done without lunch it would be all cleaned up.

Shannon and I requested a table for two in the garden restaurant; it was quaint and underused by the cruisers. The white rod iron tables and chairs were nestled in their own beautiful section surrounded by plants in hanging baskets, flowers cascading down to create divide, and water flowing through creating a soft music throughout. This was much what I imagined the ancient gardens of Babylon were like at least I hoped they were. 'I hoped they brought people peace like this does for me. Thomas and I use to talk about all the places we wished we could visit that no longer exist. Why was I thinking about this right now?' My stupid brain had wondered off into its own place again. I needed to focus on my current predicament.

"I am so sorry I didn't tell you about my relationship with Tom. We decided it was better not to disclose our relationship until Alena was home. I felt so bad lying to you after you were so nice." Shannon started. This was the most she had spoken our entire journey. She was generally reserved but had a very kind soul.

"Please I'm not mad. It might go without saying now, but I am no stranger to secrets. I would love to hear your story though. You are very beautiful and endearing when you're together." I smiled. It actually felt nice to have a normal conversation. This was the first one we had the entire trip.

"Well, we met five years ago Tom was looking for silks in Indonesia and I was finding myself or something supposedly. He really hasn't changed much. He was the same kind gently soul he is now. We got engaged last summer and were due to be married last month. We put things on hold because Alena..."

Just as she finished her statement the GPS tracker started beeping and Tom came running in. The lights went out and we could hear gun fire in the distance.

"Pirates... The captain ... People." Tom stopped for a moment as he reached us. "Pirates are aboard the ship. They seem to be searching for something aboard." Tom finally finished as we creeped down the wall and into a storage area next to the kitchen.

"I think I know what they want. The GPS trackers are showing movement in the antiquities' boxes. It looks as if they are being stacked to the wall closest to the cargo elevator." I whispered. "We must be getting close to the bay."

Tom squatted and started moving towards the back of the ship. "We have to get to the back of the boat so we can follow when they unload them." Tom expressed with great concern. "If we lose them, they will be gone forever as will my Alena." His voice trailed off at the end of his sentence. We kept moving out of the garden restaurant and to the right.

We came to the first hallway of rooms towards the middle of the desk. A guard with two automatic weapons was patrolling. A little opening to the cleaning coset kept us secure until he passed. Tom gestured for us to follow as he took us down the long hallway. Once we reached the back of ship, he began trying doors along the wall until we found one open. The porthole window on the back wall allowed us to see a small boat with two men follow us just above the cargo elevator's opening.

"Now what?" Shannon whispered.

"Nothing to do but wait and see. We can't move on the collection until we see Alena or arrive at shore. We will take turns watching and tracking GPS until something happens." I replied. We ransacked the room looking for snacks and chargers. I felt bad taking people's stuff but didn't have a choice. We waited and waited. I thought they would move at nightfall, but they didn't, so we took turns watching and sleeping.

The next morning, we heard arguing in the hall outside our room. They were yelling in an ancient language that I had only heard spoken one time before. I didn't understand any of it, but I knew it was the same as Thomas spoke on the phone before his last trip to Turkey. I was the language of my Thomas's killer. These guys were somehow connected to the tribe that killed my love. None of this makes sense. Then we heard knocks on a couple doors in the hallway and shots fired. We quickly hid in the bathtub and locked the bathroom door. After what seemed like days, it was probably only a couple hours, we started feeling the boat rock a lot followed by a loss of power.

"Perfect. The storm has come in." I whispered. The GPS still showed the collection on the back wall of the ship although it was sliding around as the waves rocked. The largest wave yet rolled the boat way on its left side. I could hear metal splitting and water rushing. All of the sudden everything was chaos. Pitch black. Water rolling over us. Tumbling everywhere.   Bang. My head crashed into the side of the bathtub we had once been hiding in. I black out into nothingness. Everything was empty my mind, my body, all floating effortlessly lost.

Back to Reality.

"That's when we woke up on the beach." Shannon replied as we sat in the cove behind the rocks. "These are the pirated that boarded our ship. We are waiting on someone who is coming to retrieve your collection."

"Oh I... I think I do remember. I know what we have to do next. We have to find those boxes and retag the GPS. They should still be active." I replied as all the memories started flooding back to me.

Shannon hugged me tightly around the neck. "I'm so glad you ok. We need you." She smiled as she held back tears.

Meet me back here after dinner. I'll show you where the boxes are. We must go." Shannon left the cave first and head back towards the kitchen to make dinner. I walked back towards the shelter where Cheryl had woken me. A thought got stuck in my mind at that point 'Watch Cheryl. Something is off.' I had no idea why I suddenly felt so negatively about Cheryl. I had barely seen her the entire trip and when I did, she was perfectly pleasant. Yet, her name created knots in my stomach.

Her perfect appearance when we first washed up on the beach bothered me, but it was more than that. As I rattled everything that had happened around in my brain, I was suddenly struck by the fact she had never shown fear. All of us had fear in our eyes at one point or another. Shannon in the kitchen, Tom on the beach but not Cheryl. When I first reached her on the beach, she seemed frustrated, and I mistook it for fear. When I woke up here at the in the shelter, she was pleasant and unscathed. She must know she's ok. She's in on it. That's how they got to Tom and possibly me.

As I arrived at the shelter, I decided my best option was to play the game. I needed no one to suspect how much I was piecing together. I needed to stay ahead of the game. Cheryl and another man whom I did not know were standing in the tent having a discussion in hushed tones.

"Hello, I don't mean to interrupt." I said sweetly trying to sound naïve. "I see everyone doing things here. Is there a system to helping? Is there something I can do?" I remained calm and steady on the outside but inside I was crawling. I wanted to yell and scream and let everyone know who the snake really was.

"Oh, you must be feeling better dear. We are just trying to establish a base and survival until we can get another ship home. Tom has been trying to find a way to reach authorities with the locals since this morning. Maybe try the kitchen. I'm sure those ladies could use help." Cheryl watched until I was out of earshot and the turned back to the man. I needed to keep my eye on them. I think they are very involved.

As I entered the kitchen, I made eye contact with Shannon. She was slicing fruit with a woman from the tribe. There were several groups of women having different conversations about life. As a I picked up a piece of fruit to wash it Shannon introduced me to Nia, the local woman she was speaking with. I kept me conversation light, but I was truly digging into who exactly these people were. Finally, I asked her about her language, and everything started to come into focus.

"My father was from Turkey. He lived in a small village that no longer exist. There was a bomb blast and fighting a few years back that made people in the village disperse. I came here with my son's friend to escape." She was innocently telling her story.

"Oh, do you like history? You are very good at telling stories." I smile as I try to prompt her for information.

"Yes." She replied. "In fact, I have only found one person who likes it more than me. A man my father brought home around the time of the bomb told us of his collection. I gave him a silver cat from our village to take to his wife. He told me all the stories of their travels and all about their collection of artifacts. Our village was so impressed" She got really quiet and sad. "The mean men on the other side of the wall hurt my friend very badly. I never saw him after that."

"I'm so sorry. I am sure your friend's wife loved her silver cat." I smiled trying to hide back tears. That cat was mailed to me with Thomas's last letter. He told me all about the beautiful little girl who shared it with him. He wanted our future daughter to be just like her. She was very lovely and kind. It took me back for a moment but once again I needed to remind myself to focus. 'That's how they found out about the collection. I thought as I continued chopping. Shannon shot me a quick glance. I nodded to reassure her I was ok.

We finished dinner and served a picnic style meal under the evening sky. The sunset was beautiful, almost painted. I took the opportunity in inquire about their lives without pushing or interrogating. I need information but didn't want to spoke them in to shutting down. I really was interested in their stories. I loved learning about new places and people. Finally, after stuffing myself I decided it was time to meet Shannon. I started off on a walk down the beach to clear my head, at least that is what I had told those who inquired. I climbed over the rocks and back into the cove to wait.

Shannon appeared approximately ten minutes later with Tom in tow. I hugged him and was thankful he was there. It was time to set forth a plan and get us back on track. We needed to find Alena, stop the smuggler's, and get home.

"The crates are being kept in a back tent and so is Alena. I saw glimpses of her when I snuck back there but was not able to get to her" Tom had on his serious face as he spoke, but the glimmer of hope was still present in his eyes.

"I have an idea, but it will take a lot of moving pieces. Also, we need to watch Cheryl. She is involved."

"I knew it" Tom said. "There is no way they could have known without an inside man. Don recommended her for the job, so I trusted him." Tom looked defeated. Cheryl knows all the ends and outs. She could really do damage.

"Don't worry. I think I heard Cheryl and the guy she was talking to say the coast guard would be here tomorrow, but they are moving the antiquities tonight. We are going to make sure we are on the ship with the crates. Don't panic." I assured Tom and Shannon. "Follow my lead."

We crept back into the forest under the cover of darkness. Every time a branch snapped, or a leave crunched my heart raced. This was our one chance to save Alena and my collection. We had to do it right. Just outside of the camp where they were holding Alena we stopped and built a small covering out of leaves to help hide us. We sat in silence for what felt like eternity before movement really started to pick up at the camp. Then an older model army style truck pulled in and the crates were loaded in the back. Alena was moved into the back of the truck and tied to the railing. The two men and Cheryl went into a building nearby.

"Now is our chance. We need to get Alena and come back into the jungle. The trackers are still active on the crates so we can follow those after." I whispered. I slipped over to spy on the men through the windows while Tom cut Alena free from the railing. She looked tired and worn down but not too shabby for a captive.

"We got to go. They are almost finished." I stated with urgency. We scurried back into the cover of jungle with Alena in tow. We had to get far away from the truck and the men. They would look for her as soon as they noticed her missing. Once we reached the shore, we held up in a cave just to the right of the dock.

"Oh Alena, are you ok? Did they hurt you?" Toms' arms were wrapped so tight I don't think he would ever let go.

"I'm fine. Those men are selling a treasure to Dr. Fiseman. He told them it they would get it for him he would pay them lots of money. I overheard them on the phone." Alena was so proud for remembering the name. I could tell she was scared but she had on a brave face.

"Are you sure they said Fiseman?" I suddenly felt like I was going to pass out. Dr. Fiseman had been on Thomas' last trip. He was the only other American with Thomas and knew what the antiquities were worth.

"I'm positive." She replied. Just then we heard shouting in the distance. They must have discovered Alena missing. We need to sit tight and be silent until the ship comes in. We curl up in the back of the cave hearing rustling all around us. I am not sure how we avoided detection, but we did. About two hours later a ship came in from the east.

"Wake up! They must be moving the treasure now." I tapped on each of the members of the group as I continued talking. "They will come to shore for fuel and that is when we make our move. Not all of us should go just in case. Someone should wait on the coast guard here."

Tom looked anxious and quickly replied "Shannon, stay with Alena. Have the Coast Guard give her a once over and let them know what is going on. I'm going to slip out and get the information off the ship then we will get on it. Hopefully they can track it."

I could already see the tears in Shannon's eyes as Tom crept out to get the information. "Look I promise I will talk care of him. We will get you your life back." She nodded still upset but with understanding of what was necessary. Tom came back in and reported the ship info to Shannon. We all shared a final hug and then it was time to split off.

The End or The Beginning,

Tom and I slipped over to behind some barrels just off the dock until the last crew had departed the ship. We could hear them talking about a quick dinner before departing. This was our chance to hide.

We scurried around the barrels and out on to the dock walking up an incline to board. It was not as big as the cruise ship we came over on, but it was definitely a good size ship. We came into a series of stairwells and a long hallway to the back of the boat.

"We need to go down at least one level so they can't immediately find us when they come back." Tom whispered.

"Agreed but we shouldn't go all the way to the bottom either." I responded. We went down the hallway slowly trying doors. The third door on the left opened to a small unused sleeping quarters with plenty of places to hide. One tiny window above the bunk allowed us to tell if it was day or night. The real problem was I had no idea what to do next. We stayed with the treasure, but our only hope was Shannon and Alena alerting the coast guard. If we got to the drop and no coast guard was there, we had no back up plan.

Would we just keep following this treasure forever? As night settled in so did we.

At first light Shannon heard the waves crashing against a large ship near the beach. She crawled from the cave pulling Alena to the edge of the water. “Over here.” She screamed and waved her arms frantically. “Please we need you hear.” The distinct boat, white trimmed in red, immediately let her know the coast guard had finally arrived. She could see the first men coming ashore.

“Please” She screamed once more. “We need medical treatment, and you need to go get the stolen treasure.” The two men in front of her looked as if she'd grown extra heads. She needed to explain in a much better way. Then she remembered the GPS chips. "Hurry let me see your phone." Shannon began giving detailed information to get the coast guard on board.

Back on the treasure ship morning light was breaking through the window. I could hear a few conversations in the hallway outside our room. Apparently, we were only about three hours out from our destination. I was praying that Shannon had reached the Coast Guard by now. We were about probably about 2 hours ahead of them based on when we dropped anchor and the expected time of their arrival back at the island. We were not yet moving which would give them some time to catch up. Now we just wait and wait and wait.

Tom and I took turns resting and standing guard. We didn't know when it would happen, but we knew at some point we may no longer have the opportunity. As I started my second shift, I heard a long loud whistle in the distance. I peaked my head up just enough to glimpse out the window. Another boat seemed to be pulling up close to us. It was smaller than a cruise ship but larger than a fishing boat. I could see a few cargo containers on the deck.

“Tom” I whispered nudging his side. “Tom, Look outside.” Just as Tom stood up the boat gave a violent rock and a large commotion happened in the hall.

“Stay still and stay down.” Tom replied.

“Start the transfer.” “You don’t tell me what to do” Random yelling and gun fire could be heard from the hall. Just as this happened a second harsh waive then a third rocked the boat violently.

“NO ONE MOVE. THE COST GUARD IS BOARDING BOTH VESSELS”

Tom and I looked at each other tears streaming down our faces. Finally, we could leave this to the professionals. No more tracking or tracing or worrying about loved ones. We were saved.

"Follow me out. Keep your hands visible and be ready to give all the information." Tom gave me a nod and we slowly opened the door. As we entered the hallway there was no one in sight. We moved back towards the stairs we had climbed down to get there. Just as we reached the bottom the black barrel of a weapon was in our face. We could see a coast guard officer at the other end.

"Please sir, I'm Tom and this is Kat. We sent Shannon to find you. We need you to help us recover the stolen antiquities" Tom was talking so quickly I wasn't sure the officer could even understand him.

Just then the officer grabbed his radio and remarked "We have the hostages sir. She was telling the truth. I am bringing them to your office now."

Relief was spreading through out my body as we followed the officer to the captain. I wasn't actually sure we would ever be rescued. Honestly, I was out of plans. I had no moves if the coast guard didn't show. I told myself I was protecting a legacy but really, I was a sitting duck out of moves and I had dragged Tom into it with me.

The officer took us to the captain's office where recounted details of the past few days. The captain was in awe of our story and our bravery. I bet he was really thinking our stupidity for getting on the ship. We watched as the treasure along with many other hostages were removed from the ship. This process took several hours. They asked me to assist in going through boxes and accounting for all the stolen antiquities. Apparently, this was a ring of human trafficking and theft the

Coast Guard had been trying to get their hands on for over a year. Finally, once all was accounted for and arrest were made, we set sail for home.

I was so excited to see my family, but I had some obvious explaining to do. I just prayed that they would forgive me for the secrets of the treasures. Also, I wanted to make sure Tom, Shannon, and Alena would be ok. They had become like part of my family as well.

Tom and I stood on the deck, breeze blowing in our faces, as we pulled into port. We didn't say much to each other but there was nothing that needed said. We knew we were forever connected and forever thankful. I could see our families before we ever reached the dock. Tears would not stop running down my face. I hugged my husband and children as if I would never let go.

"Thank you." Shannon was teary eyed as she through her arms around me.

"Always" I replied. We chatted and made the necessary introductions before going our separate ways but promised to keep in touch.

In the car I took a deep breath before explaining all that had happened. I told the stories of Thomas Allen, our marriage, and travels. My husband was a little taken back but understood why I had not mentioned it before. Then he said the most shocking thing from the entire trip. He already knew about Thomas. In his work several years ago, he had met a girl I went to grad school with, and she told him she was glad I found someone after Thomas. He never said a word to me, but he knew. It made me wonder how long I had been taking advantage of this wonderful man. Then he drove me not home but to the University museum. I gave him a puzzled look.

"Don't you think it's about time you let us in on your adventures?" He smiled.

Tears welled up in my eyes as I mouthed, I love you. "I think you kids would love to know about their mother and the man who inspired her."

I couldn't believe it. I finally was able to share my treasure with the most important people in my life. Thomas had left my family a beautiful gift and it was time I start letting them experience it.

Three months later, we flew as a family to Tennessee for Tom and Shannon's wedding. Alena was living with them and recovering from her trauma. Tom, Shannon, and Alena will visit us in a few months. I can truly say they are now extended family. Although how we had met was something out of a movie, I don't regret it for a second. I was so glad to share in this beautiful moment with such special people. It is because of my unfortunate side hustle experience that my family is stronger than ever, and my priorities have become clear. I spend my days at the museum sharing all our worldly adventures and have added artifacts from Alena's rescue to remind people what to look out for. My evenings are by far my favorite whether it be hockey or homework we do all of it as a family.

While I really want to end the story there, I am sure you have some questions, so here is the quick rundown. Cheryl and the other captors all received hundreds of years in prison for human trafficking. Thirty-four hostages were removed from the ship and returned to their families. Another one hundred twenty-five were traced and are currently being located. 1.8 Billion dollars in illegal antiquities trades were recovered and returned to museums across the world. Each time I tell the story I hope a few more hostages are saved and a few more stories uncovered.

www.ingramcontent.com/pod-product-compliance
Lightning Source LLC
LaVergne TN
LVHW041104150826
845673LV00007B/1915

* 9 7 9 8 7 5 5 0 1 6 5 5 1 *